W9-AOL-906

*To Yuyi Morales, for her good critiques and friendship —S. E.*

*Para Jamie, mi ángel de Navidad —M. B.*

*Para mis primos y primas, con amor —J. C.*

Text © 2007 by Susan Middleton Elya and Merry Banks.
Illustrations © 2007 by Joe Cepeda.

Book design by Mariana Oldenburg.
Typeset in Cochin and Khaki.
The illustrations in this book were rendered in oils and acrylic on illustration board.
Manufactured in China.

Library of Congress Cataloging-in-Publication Data
Elya, Susan Middleton, 1955–
N is for Navidad / by Susan Middleton Elya and Merry Banks ; illustrated by Joe Cepeda.
p. cm.
Summary: A rhyming book that outlines the preparations for and celebration of the Christmas season,
with Spanish words for each letter of the alphabet translated in a glossary.
ISBN-13: 978-0-8118-5205-0
ISBN-10: 0-8118-5205-9
[1. Christmas—Fiction. 2. Hispanic Americans—Fiction. 3. Alphabet.
4. Spanish language—Fiction. 5. Stories in rhyme.]  I. Banks, Merry.
II. Cepeda, Joe, ill.  III. Title.
PZ8.3.E514Naai 2007
[E]—dc22
2006008169

Distributed in Canada by Raincoast Books
9050 Shaughnessy Street, Vancouver, British Columbia V6P 6E5

10 9 8 7 6 5 4 3 2 1

Chronicle Books LLC
680 Second Street, San Francisco, California 94107

www.chroniclekids.com

# N Is for Navidad

By Susan Middleton Elya
& Merry Banks

Illustrated by Joe Cepeda

chronicle books · san francisco

A is for **ángel**,
hung high by Papá.

B is for buñuelos,
fried by Mamá.

**C** is for **campanas**,

at the church down the street.

**CH** is for **chiles**,
to string, not to eat!

'D is for **dulces**,
a sweet preparation.

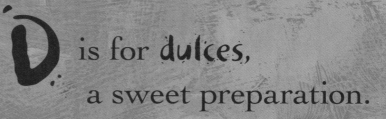

# E is for estrella,
## a bright decoration.

**F** is for
**flor de Nochebuena,**
so pretty.

G is for *gente*,
     the folks in our city.

H is for **hogar**.
Las Posadas begin.
At each house they say,
"No room at the inn."

**I** is for **iglesia**,
   our beautiful church.
      We pass it each night
         as we go on our search.

**J** is for **José**,
María by his side.

**K** is for **kilómetros**,
the travelers' long ride.

**L** is for **luminarias**. Hurray!
They're paper-bagged candles
that light up the way.

**Ll** is for **llegada**,
the arrival to Earth.
In just four more days,
we'll honor His birth.

**M** is for **mantilla**
that Abuela will wear,
a lacy black scarf
to cover her hair.

Ñ is for the **nacimiento** we've made.
Ñ is for **niño**. He'll soon be displayed.

At midnight we all head to church for la misa.
At last! ¡Navidad! Each mouth, a sonrisa.

# O is for ojos.
Just look at the food!
Deep-fried and baked
and roasted and stewed.

**P** is pesebre
where Jesus was born
and also **pan dulce**
we eat in the morn.

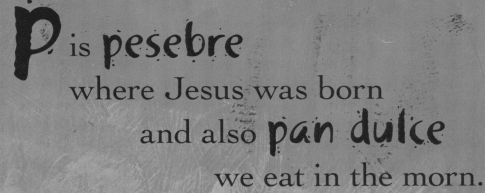

Q is for **quesadillas**—delicious.
Tía has cooked them,
so guess who does dishes!

:R is for **risas**.
We laugh at the joke.
Tío has tricked us again.
We're still broke!

**Rr** is for **arroz** to go with the beans.
Company's coming. We know what that means.

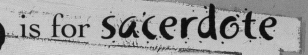

**S** is for **sacerdote** who's here as our guest. He's joined us for supper. We're acting our best.

**T** is for **tamales**, our New Year's Eve treat.

**U** is for **uvas**, the twelve that we'll eat.

There's one for each month
of the upcoming year.
We eat them all quickly.
¡Salud! And good cheer!

**V** is for **ventana**.
We look to the sky

and pick out the star
that the kings traveled by.

W is for wise men,
**tres reyes**, three kings,

X is for **excelente**,
the feeling He brings!

Y is for **yerba**, the camels' main dish.

Z is for **zapatos**, so we'll get our wish.

We set them outside and the wise men come through
    with presents and candy and blessings for you.
        A long wait till next time to find a posada.
        But what could be better than Christmastime?

¡Nada!

# Authors' Note

Many families of Latino heritage begin celebrating the Christmas season on December 16. They continue through Christmas Day to January 6, when the three kings arrived to welcome baby Jesus. The customs featured in this book are primarily Mexican.

Several days of preparation lead up to the beginning of Las Posadas, the nine nights of processions through the streets, reenacting Joseph and Mary's search for lodging. Families and friends pretend to look for lodging, carrying candles and singing carols as they go from door to door. Each night ends with the "travelers" being admitted inside to a small party. On the last night, Christmas Eve, the families are once again let inside the last house where they enjoy the biggest party with delicious food, punch, and the breaking of the piñata.

**Abuela** (ah-BWEH-lah) Grandmother.

**Ángel** (AHN-hehl) Angel.

**Arroz** (ah-RROCE) Rice, an important side dish in many Latino households.

**Buñuelos** (boo-NYWEH-loce) Flat, fried pastries, sprinkled with sugar and cinnamon.

**Campanas** (kahm-PAH-nahs) Bells.

**Chiles** (CHEE-lehs) Peppers. Dried chiles strung for decoration are a common sight in fall and winter in the American Southwest.

**Dulces** (DOOL-sehs) Candy. Dulces are made in preparation for company, parties, and the celebration of Christmas. They include *pan dulce, leche quemada,* candied oranges and sweet potatoes, pumpkin candies, pecan pralines, coconut candies, and peanut patties.

**Estrella** (ehs-TREH-yah) Star. A star is the traditional shape of a Christmas Eve piñata, a papier-mâché vessel filled with candies and small toys.

**Excelente** (ehk-seh-LEHN-teh) Excellent.

**Flor de Nochebuena** (FLOHR DEH noe-cheh-BWEH-nah) Poinsettia. Flor de Nochebuena is native to Mexico. Mexican folklore says that a little girl discovered the flower when she was looking for a gift for Jesus, and that she took it to the church on December 24.

**Gente** (HEHN-teh) People.

**Hogar** (oe-GAHR) Home. During Las Posadas, "travelers" go from home to home, eventually being admitted inside on the last night. Friends and relatives answer the travelers' song with another song, saying that they may stay there for the night.

**Iglesia** (ee-GLEH-syah) Church.

**José** (ho-SEH) Joseph, Mary's husband.

**Kilómetros** (kee-LOE-meh-troce) A metric measurement equivalent to 1,000 meters.

**Luminarias** (loo-mee-NAH-ryahs) Bags of sand with candles inside that line the road to light the way. This tradition dates back to sixteenth-century Spain.

**Llegada** (yeh-GAH-dah) Arrival.

**Mantilla** (mahn-TEE-yah) Veil or headscarf worn by older women in the Catholic church.

**María** (mah-REE-ah) Mary, mother of Jesus.

**Misa** (MEE-sah) Mass.

**Nacimiento** (nah-see-MYEHN-toe) Nativity scene. To a Catholic family of Latino heritage this is often more important than a Christmas tree. The cradle is empty until midnight on Christmas Eve.

**Nada** (NAH-dah) Nothing.

**Navidad** (nah-vee-DAHD) Christmas.

**Niño** (NEE-nyoe) Infant (in this case the baby Jesus).

**Ojos** (OE-hoce) Eyes.

**Pan dulce** (PAHN DOOL-seh) A sweet bread coated with a sugar and egg mixture, made fresh for special occasions, including Christmas.

**Pesebre** (peh-SEH-breh) Manger.

**Posada** (poe-SAH-dah) Inn.

**Quesadillas** (keh-sah-DEE-yahs) Fried or grilled tortillas with melted cheese.

**Risas** (RREE-sahs) Laughter. December 28 is el Día de los Inocentes—like April Fool's Day. Pranks and jokes are played, like the one involving a $20 bill with a string attached to it. The kids reach for the bill, and Tío pulls the string and snatches back the money.

**Sacerdote** (sah-sehr-DOE-teh) Priest.

**Salud** (sah-LOOD) To your health.

**Sonrisa** (sone-REE-sah) Smile.

**Tamales** (tah-MAH-lehs) Dough made of corn flour then filled with meat, vegetables, or fruit. Tamales are steamed in corn husks and served as a special treat on holidays.

**Tía** (TEE-ah) Aunt.

**Tío** (TEE-oh) Uncle.

**Tres reyes** (TREHS RREH-yehs) Three kings. The three wise men followed the bright star and traveled on camels for 12 days to reach the manger in Bethlehem where Jesus was born. Three Kings Day is celebrated January 6.

**Uvas** (OO-vahs) Grapes. Twelve grapes are traditionally eaten in the first minute after midnight on New Year's Eve for good luck. This custom comes from Spain.

**Ventana** (vehn-TAH-nah) Window.

**Yerba** (YEHR-bah) Grass (also spelled hierba). Latino children put grass in their shoes for the three kings' camels the night before Three Kings Day.

**Zapatos** (sah-PAH-toce) Shoes. The children set out shoes the night before Three Kings Day, so that the three wise men can leave them a gift. For this fiesta, many families make *rosca de reyes*, a ring-shaped bread with a tiny doll baked inside. Whoever gets the lucky slice with the doll will host a party in the future.